YuMee

Recipes for Young Chefs

Aoileann Garavaglia

BLACKWATER PRESS

Editor
Sinéad Lawton

Design/Cover
Liz Murphy

Photography
Declan Corrigan

Food Stylist
Sheila Rasmussen

Illustrations
Bronagh O'Hanlon

Produced in Ireland by
Blackwater Press
c/o Folens Publishers
Hibernian Industrial Estate
Greenhills Road
Tallaght, Dublin 24

For mum Linda, papa Theodore, my brother Caoimhín
and grandmas Bernice and Frances
with a bellyful of love.

Acknowledgements

A big thank you to the team involved in making this book: my editors Margaret Burns and Sinéad Lawton for their patience, Liz Murphy for the design, Declan Corrigan for his mouth-watering pictures and John O'Connor for being helpful and understanding.

A special thank you to Bronagh O'Hanlon for making this book full of visual humour and to Marcus Lynam for introducing me to Bronagh.

This also gives me the opportunity to show my appreciation for the wonderful support I received in making the TV series YUMee. A big thank you to John Williams, series producer of YUMee, Sheila Rasmussen, food advisor, Kevin Linehan, David Donaghy, Michael Croke of CEL, all my colleagues in the Young People's Department of RTÉ, and the Den 2 gang for all their help and support in making the TV series YUMee. Thank you also to Ciara O'Donnell for the set design, Shirley Dalton for the graphic design, Michelle Steins for organising and buying all of the goods, and to all the crews with whom I worked.

Last but not least many thanks to my family and friends: Mum, Caoimhín, Granny, Kathleen Morris and family, Beek Grosh and family, Kari Rocca and family, Mary Kingston and Brian Graham, Pearse Lehane, and Aidan Power, without whose loving friendship and support this book would never have happened.

A big go raibh míle maith agat to Papa for putting up with me.

Contents

Le bia maith teagann saol breá

Weights, Measures and Servings

Sometimes you may have a weighing scales or measuring jug that measures things out in a different way than they are done in this book. If you do, you can work out how much of something you need from the charts below, a grown-up will be able to help you. Remember never to mix metric (on the left) and imperial (on the right) measures in a recipe!

Solids		Liquids	
Metric	Imperial	Metric	Imperial
15 g	½ oz	5 ml	1 teaspoon
30 g	1 oz	15 ml	1 tablespoon
50 g	1⅔ oz	150 ml	¼ pint
150 g	5 oz	300 ml	½ pint
300 g	10 oz	600 ml	1 pint
480 g	16 oz (1 lb)	1 litre	1¾ pints
720 g	1½ lb	1.1 litres	2 pints
1 kg	2 lb 1⅓ oz	250 ml	1 cup

* Always use weighing scales to weigh amounts carefully.
* Use the table provided to help you.
* A 'pinch of salt or pepper' is the amount you can hold between your thumb and your first finger.
* When you measure with spoons they should be level, not heaped. A good trick is to fill the spoon and then level off using the edge of the table knife.
  You can get metric measuring spoons which are easy to use and very accurate.

Oven Temperatures

All ovens are different and cooking times are only a guide. Get into the habit of touching and looking at food to find out if it is properly cooked.

Gas Mark	Centigrade	Farenheit	
¼	80°C	175°F	Cool
½	110°C	225°F	
1	130°C	250°F	
2	150°C	300°F	
3	170°C	325°F	Moderate
4	180°C	350°F	
5	190°C	375°F	
6	200°C	400°F	
7	220°C	425°F	Hot
8	230°C	450°F	Very Hot

> NEVER USE AN OVEN, COOKER OR MICROWAVE WITHOUT THE HELP OF AN ADULT.

Kitchen Safety

* Always let a grown-up know when you are going to work in the kitchen.
* Never use sharp knives. Always use a table knife and have a grown-up with you when you are using it. If you have any difficulties, ask an adult to cut the ingredients for you.
* Always cut the ingredients on a chopping board and cut away from you.
* Use hand-operated kitchen appliances rather than electrical appliances. If you have to use an electric appliance, get an adult to do it for you.
* Never go near the oven, cooker or microwave without an adult helper. Always get the adult to put things in the oven and to take them out again. Be very careful because containers can be very hot.

* Always use a clean cloth to wipe the work surface.
* Wash all fruit and vegetables.
* Never taste with your fingers, use a spoon.
* Keep all pets out of the kitchen.
* Leave enough time to cook and clean up.
* The recipes in this book were written for you, but it is always a good idea to show the recipe to an adult before you start to cook.

Emergency numbers   999

Local Gardaí   _____
Mum work   _____
Dad work   _____
Family members   _____
Neighbour   _____
Friend   _____

Before you start

* Always wear an apron or smock before you start to cook to protect your clothing and for safety.
* Tie back your hair if you need to.
* Wash your hands before and after you handle food. Use an antibacterial washing liquid when washing your hands to prevent any spread of germs. Food can carry lots of germs and it's best to prevent germs from spreading to other food.
* Read the whole recipe through to make sure you have all the ingredients and tools you need.
* Clear a work area before you start.
* Carefully weigh or measure all the ingredients you use.

While you are cooking

* Get an adult to put things in and take things out of the oven.
* Always get an adult to handle hot dishes.
* Follow the recipe step by step.

And After

* Wash the dishes.
* Clean up spills and crumbs on the counter and floor.
* Wipe down the surfaces with a hot, soapy dishcloth.
* Put all the extra ingredients away.
* Store food in a proper container and at the correct temperatures. If something needs to be kept cold then store it in the fridge.
* Make sure your adult helper checks to see if the oven, grill, cooker and microwave are switched off.

Leave the kitchen clean and tidy

Some of the recipes in this book contain nuts. Some people are allergic to nuts and aren't allowed to eat them. Ask an adult if it is safe for you to eat nuts.
If nuts are used in a recipe you will see this symbol.

A Word from the Author

You may already know me from my TV programme *YUMee*, or from Den 2 and TG4. Like my name, which is both Gaelic and Italian, my love of cooking comes from the same two traditions. During my childhood, I learned on Inis Meáin from Bean an Tigh the love of fresh country baking. From Mummy, I learned the importance of caution and cleanliness in the kitchen. Papa, who thinks chile is a breakfast dish, taught me that food presentation can be both artistic and funny. Granny, who learned from Mama Angelina the spicy secrets of Lombardia, taught me the delights of flavour and aroma. From my brother, whose specialty is gourmet delicacies, I learned the rewards to be reaped from patience and preparation.

Among my personal favourites are the soups and desserts, especially the chocolate ones, of the Swiss Alps, and the flavoursome fish dishes from the west of Ireland and the south of France. I hope you find in this book some of the love and pleasure I have found in creating food to share with family and friends.

Dia libh
Buon Appetito

YUMee

Recipes

Chocolate Biscuit

You will need

150g biscuits
  (digestives or
  lady fingers)
250g best quality
  chocolate (70% cocoa)
50g butter
25g jelly sweets
1 cup cream

Tools

3 large mixing bowls
dish that can go in the
  microwave
non-stick tin (loaf tin
  works best)
chopping board
table knife
whisk
wooden spoon
dessertspoon
spatula
weighing scales

1 Break up the biscuits into large chunks and put them into a mixing bowl.

2 Use a table knife to cut the jelly sweets into bite size pieces and mix them in with the biscuits.

CHOCOLATE SAUCE

Cake

3 Put the chocolate and butter into another mixing bowl and, with the help of a grown-up, melt them in the microwave at a low heat for about 3 minutes. Keep watching the mixture in the microwave because you don't want the butter to burn. Stop it after 1½ minutes and give it a good stir. Leave it aside to cool a little because you are going to mix it with the cream.

4 In another mixing bowl whisk the cream until it becomes thick. Add the chocolate and butter mixture to the cream and give the mixture a good stir with a wooden spoon.

5 Mix the biscuit and the chocolate mixtures together until the biscuits are covered.

6 Scoop the mixture into a non-stick tin and, using the back of a dessert spoon, mash it into the tin. Really pack it in. Now place this in the fridge for 4 hours. It might be a good idea to leave it overnight.

7 Remove the cake from the fridge and use a spatula to prise around the edges to loosen it from the tin. Then tip the cake out onto a board. Use a table knife to slice.

Serve with cream and fruit or just a large glass of milk.

TIP
STRUGGLING WITH TRYING TO GET THE CAKE OUT OF THE TIN? THERE MUST BE AN EASIER WAY!

HERE'S A GREAT TIP. BEFORE YOU EMPTY THE MIXTURE INTO THE TIN, LINE THE TIN WITH SOME CLING FILM, AND THE CAKE WILL JUST LIFT OUT.

Cinnamon Roll

These always keep the cookie monster happy!!

You will need

250g flour
250g butter
115g white sugar
1 egg yolk

To decorate
1 dessertspoon cinnamon
3 dessertspoons sugar
1 egg white

Tools

2 mixing bowls
wooden spoon
sieve
2 airtight plastic bags
dinner plate
chopping board
table knife
non-stick baking tray
wire rack
weighing scales

1 Put the butter into a mixing bowl and leave it to sit out at room temperature for about half an hour until it becomes soft. This makes it easier to cream.

2 Add the sugar to the butter and give them a good mix using a wooden spoon. The mixture should become thick and creamy with no lumps.

3 Mix the egg yolk in with the butter and sugar.

4 Sieve in the flour a little at a time and keep mixing. When the mixture becomes too stiff to mix with a wooden spoon, use your fingers. Make sure to put a little flour on your fingers to stop the dough from sticking to them.

4

Cookies

5 Shape the dough into two rolls. Put the rolls into airtight plastic bags and put them in the fridge for at least one hour. This makes the dough solid and easier to work with.

6 Whisk the egg white in a mixing bowl until it is light and fluffy.

TIP
IF YOU HAVE ENOUGH COOKIES FROM ONE DOUGH ROLL, FREEZE THE OTHER ROLL FOR ANOTHER DAY.

7 Mix the sugar and cinnamon on a dinner plate.

8 Take the dough out of the fridge and roll in the egg white until it is coated. Then roll it in the cinnamon and sugar.

9 Place the dough on a chopping board and, using a table knife, cut the dough into slices. Make sure that they are not too thick, about the same thickness as a regular biscuit is fine.

10 Put the slices of cut dough onto a non-stick baking tray.

11 Get an adult to help you put the cookies in a moderate oven, 180°C/350°F/gas mark 4, baking them for about 10 minutes. The cooking time really depends on the thickness of the cookies, the thicker they are the longer they will take. You will know they are ready when they are golden brown.

12 Get a grown-up to help you place the cookies on a wire rack to cool.

Krispie Cake

You will need

3 large Mars bars
50g butter
200g Rice Krispies
  (4 large mugfuls)

For the icing
100g dark chocolate
25g butter
1 dessertspoon cream

Tools

table knife
chopping board
dish that can be put in the
  microwave
tablespoon
mug
round cake tin
dessertspoon
wooden spoon
weighing scales

1 Using a table knife and chopping board, cut the Mars bars into chunks.

2 Put the chunks of Mars bar and 50g of butter into a dish that can be put into the microwave. Get an adult to help you to melt them at a low to medium setting in the microwave for about 3 minutes. After each minute give the mixture a stir with a tablespoon.

3 Once the mixture has melted, stir in the Rice Krispies. Add a mugful at a time, this makes it easier to mix together. Make sure all the cereal is covered with the chocolate.

4 Spread the mixture into a 6-inch non-stick round cake tin and press down using a dessertspoon.

5 With the help of a grown-up, melt 100g of dark chocolate and 25g of butter in a microwave at a low to medium setting for about 3 minutes. Add a dessertspoon of cream and stir using a wooden spoon. Now pour the icing onto the Krispie Cake.

6 Chill the cake in the fridge for about an hour. Remove and cut into finger-size bites.

You can even make the cake without the icing if you like.

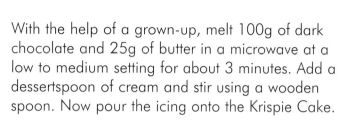

TIP
You can also make little Krispie cakes. Spoon a teaspoon of the mixture for small ones or a dessertspoon for larger ones into a paper case. Put them into an old biscuit box or plastic container and set aside for half an hour.

They all taste great with a nice glass of milk.

Dippy Dip Dip

You will need

200ml crème fraîche
200ml thick mayonnaise
1 crushed clove of garlic
2 chopped green onions
½ teaspoon curry powder
½ teaspoon paprika
1 dessertspoon ketchup

Food for dipping
celery
carrots
cucumber

Tools

large mixing bowl
garlic crusher
table knife
chopping board
tablespoon
serving bowl

1. Mix the crème fraîche and mayonnaise in a mixing bowl. It is best to use a thick mayonnaise because the dip will not stick if it is runny. Don't use salad cream or you will end up with Drippy Dip.

2. Crush the garlic using a garlic crusher, you may need a grown-up to help you. Make sure not to put your hands anywhere near your eyes after handling garlic, like onions this can really sting.

3. Using a table knife and chopping board, carefully chop the green onion into little bits.

4. Now add the curry powder, paprika and ketchup. Give it all a good mix using a tablespoon.

5. Place the dip into a nice bowl ready to serve.

6. Wash and peel some carrots, celery and a little cucumber. Use your table knife to cut them into strips for dipping. Get a grown-up to help you. You can also dip in chunks of cheese or crisps.

7. If you have any dip left over put it into a clean jar and label it. The dip will last up to 3 days in the fridge.

TIP
USE THE CONTAINER THE CRÈME FRAÎCHE COMES IN TO MEASURE OUT THE SAME AMOUNT OF MAYO. THIS WAY YOU GET EQUAL AMOUNTS OF MAYO AND CRÈME FRAÎCHE

Moomeringues

For about 20 meringues you will need

3 large egg whites
170g white castor sugar

For the filling
50g dark chocolate
1 small cup of cream

Tools

2 large mixing bowls
hand whisk
2 dessertspoons
baking paper
baking tray
mixing bowl than can be
   used in the microwave

1 Get a grown-up to preheat the oven to 130°C/ 250°F/gas mark 1, this is a very low heat.

2 Always check the best before date on the eggs before you use them. Separate the egg white from the egg yolk. The recipe for Peach Volcano explains how to do this. Put all the egg whites in a large mixing bowl. Don't throw away the egg yolks, put them in a container and store in the fridge.

3 Using a hand whisk, whisk the egg whites until they are stiff and peaked like snowcapped mountain tops.

4 Add the sugar a little at a time, about a teaspoon, and keep whisking. A secret to good meringues is to make sure the sugar is thoroughly mixed in. You will notice while mixing the sugar that the mixture becomes shiny and stiff. When the mixture becomes almost impossible to whisk, that's when it's ready to go onto a baking tray.

5 Cover the baking tray with baking paper.

6 Use 2 dessertspoons to scoop the mixture onto the baking tray. One spoon to scoop and the other to help you scrape the mixture off the first spoon. Leave a little room between each meringue as they expand when they cook.

7 Get the grown-up to put the meringues in the oven. After an hour and a half get the grown-up to turn off the oven. Leave the meringues to cool down in the oven. This will dry them out and make them crunchy.

Filling

8 Melt chocolate in the microwave at a low heat for about 3 minutes.

9 Whisk the cream in a mixing bowl until it is stiff.

10 Add the melted chocolate to the cream and use a tablespoon to mix them together.

11 After the meringues have cooled, spoon about a tablespoon of the chocolate cream onto a meringue and sandwich two of them together.

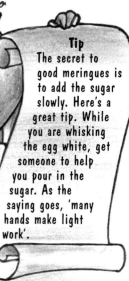

Tip
The secret to good meringues is to add the sugar slowly. Here's a great tip. While you are whisking the egg white, get someone to help you pour in the sugar. As the saying goes, 'many hands make light work'.

Cross-Oinks

You will need

1 tin of croissant
   pastry (6 croissants
   in a tin)
6 cooked sausages
6 slices of cheese
mustard
1 egg
1 tablespoon milk
pepper

Tools

chopping board
table knife
baking tray
baking paper
tablespoon
pastry brush
safety scissors
teaspoon
small mixing bowl

What do you get if you cross a croissant with a sausage?
A cross-oink!

1. Follow the instructions on the tin of uncooked croissants to get the dough out. Usually you just peel back the label and out pops the dough. Get an adult to help you if you have any problems. Roll out the dough onto a large board. Notice how each croissant is marked and use a table knife to cut along the marked edge. Each croissant is the shape of a triangle.

2. Spread one teaspoon of mustard on each triangle.

3. Put a slice of cheese on each one. Cut the cheese with a table knife if it does not fit into the triangle.

TIP
TO MAKE AN EXTRA SPECIAL TREAT, PUT 2 CHOCOLATE SQUARES IN THE CENTRE OF THE CROISSANT DOUGH. ROLL IT UP AND BAKE FOR SAME AMOUNT OF TIME.

4. Put the cooked sausage on top of the cheese at the edge of the triangle and roll it all up in the dough.

5. Line a baking tray with baking paper and put the croissants on it. To line the tray, roll out a large piece of baking paper. Place the baking tray on top of the paper and draw the outline of the tray with a pencil. Cut around the outline using safety scissors. Fold back the edges of the paper so it fits nicely in the tray.

6. Beat together an egg and a tablespoon of milk. Use a pastry brush to brush the croissants with the egg and milk. This will make them shiny and crispy on the outside.

7. Get a grown-up to preheat the oven to 200°C/400°F/gas mark 6 and cook the croissants in the oven for about 10 minutes.

You can add different fillings if you like. Try cheese and ham, cheese and spinach or even honey and banana.

Ice Cream

You will need

250ml cream
250g Greek
  yoghurt
1 dessertspoon
  sugar
1 dessertspoon
  vanilla essence
3 cups chocolate malted
  balls

Tools

large mixing bowl
whisk
airtight bag
rolling pin
lunch box
tea towel
weighing scales
wooden spoon

1 Pour the cream into a large mixing bowl and using the whisk, whisk the cream until it forms peaks.

2 Add the yoghurt, sugar and vanilla essence to the cream and mix them all together with a dessertspoon.

3 Put the chocolate malted balls into an airtight bag. Squeeze out all of the air so the bag does not burst during the next part. Place the bag on a tea towel on your work surface and give it a few wallops with a rolling pin. Don't smash them too much because you don't want them to be in smithereens, you want them in chunks.

4 Add the crushed chocolate malted balls to the creamy mixture and mix well.

5 Pour the mixture into a plastic lunch box or a clean container and place into the freezer. Leave in the freezer for 3 hours.

6 Using a dessertspoon, scoop out the ice cream into a nice serving dish, and if you like decorate with some flaked chocolate or crushed malted balls.

Instead of crushed malted balls you could add strawberries, oranges or chocolate sweets to the creamy mixture. Just use your imagination.

Oozing Oranges

You will need

5 large oranges
250g mascarpone
   cheese (an Italian
   soft sweet cheese)
175ml cream

Tools

chopping board
2 large mixing bowls
sieve
table knife
dessertspoon
wooden spoon
whisk
fork
plastic box
teaspoon
cheese grater

The best thing about Oozing Oranges is that you don't even need a bowl!!

For the best result you need an orange with a thick skin, because this makes it easier to scoop out the centre.

1 On a chopping board cut the top off the oranges with a table knife.

2 Use a dessertspoon to scoop out the centre of the oranges into a large mixing bowl.

3 In another mixing bowl whisk the cream until it is creamy rather than stiff. Add the mascarpone cheese and mix well using a wooden spoon.

4 Get a grown-up to grate the skin surface of the remaining orange. This is called zest. Add the zest to the cream and cheese.

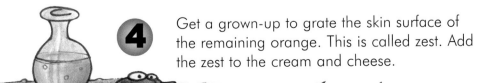

YUMee

5 Use a fork to mash up the orange that you scooped out of the orange skin and then use a sieve to strain off the juice.

6 Add about ½ cup of this orange juice to the cream and cheese mixture and mix well. You can add more juice if you like for a stronger, more orangey flavour, but be careful to keep your mixture thick and creamy.

7 Stuff the cream mixture into the orange skins and put them in a plastic box and then into the freezer for about 3 hours.

If you like you can decorate the top of the orange with a mint leaf.

TIP IF YOU HAVE ANY JUICE LEFT OVER, MAKE ORANGE ICE CUBES OR ICE lollies. POUR THE JUICE INTO THE ICE lolly mould AND PUT IN FREEZER FOR ABOUT 3 HOURS.

Peach Volcano

You will need

For four servings

2 egg whites
120g white caster
sugar
2 ripe peaches

Tools

saucer
small glass or eggcup
large mixing bowl
hand whisk
table knife
4 ramekins (little
oven-proof dishes)
dessertspoon
baking tray
teaspoon
weighing scales

To make the meringue topping

1 Check the best before date on the eggs to make sure they are fresh. Then separate the egg yolks from the egg whites (see tip). Put the egg whites into a large mixing bowl and put the yolks back in the fridge, as someone else may be able to use them.

2 Whisk the egg white until it is stiff.

3 Keep whisking, adding the sugar a little at a time. It is very important that the sugar is completely whisked in, as this is a secret to a good meringue. The mixture should at this stage become shiny and stiffen.

4 Make sure the peaches are soft and, using a table knife, cut them into halves, using ½ peach for each Peach Volcano.

Tip
Separating the egg can be a little tricky so here's a tip to make it easier. Crack the egg into a saucer. Place an eggcup over the yolk to trap it. Carefully pour the egg white into a bowl. Hey presto! The egg white has been separated from the egg yolk.

5 Place ½ peach in the bottom of each little ramekin. Scoop about 2 dessertspoons of meringue on top until the ramekin is full. Place the ramekins onto a baking tray. This just makes it easy to put them in the oven.

6 Get a grown-up to preheat the oven to a moderate temperature, 170°C/325°F/gas mark 3. Bake in the oven for about 20 minutes.

7 When the Peach Volcanoes have finished baking, leave them aside to cool for a little while because the peaches and the dish will be hot. After they cool, dig in!

Pizza!

Guarda la stella, ma guarda la Pizza più bella!

To make the dough you will need

1 packet of dried yeast
1 dessertspoon sugar
pinch of salt
1 cup with ½ warm water and ½ milk
2 dessertspoons sunflower oil
3 to 4 cups strong white flour

To make the topping you will need

140g tomato purée (from a tube)
1 dessertspoon olive oil
½ teaspoon Italian seasoning
1 crushed clove of garlic
some mozzarella cheese
olives
red and green peppers

Tools

chopping board
2 mixing bowls
wooden spoon
cling film
rolling pin
non-stick baking tray
dessertspoon
garlic crusher
table knife

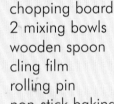

To make the dough

1 Put the yeast, sugar, salt and the cup with milk and water in a mixing bowl and stir them all together. Make sure the water is lukewarm as this will help the yeast to rise.

2 Add the oil to the bowl and mix well with a wooden spoon. Do not add the oil before this stage because if you do the yeast will stick together and the mixture won't rise.

3 Add 2 cups of strong white flour. At this stage you might find it a little difficult to mix so instead of using a wooden spoon use your hands. If you think that the mixture is too sticky just add a little more flour.

4 Now knead the bread in the bowl using your knuckles. Once you have formed a dough ball, remove it from the bowl and continue to knead on a flat work surface using some flour to stop it sticking. Push and fold for about 5 minutes until it is soft and elastic and has a silky texture.

5 Place the dough back in the bowl, cover with cling film and leave sitting in a warm place for about 2 hours. Watch it rise!!

6 Once it has risen, remove the cling film and give the dough a few good punches, knocking out all the air. Remove the dough from the bowl and knead again for a couple of minutes, pushing and folding all the time.

7 Divide the dough ball into quarters and use one for your pizza. Roll out the dough ball to make the pizza base, using a rolling pin and some flour to stop it sticking. Put the pizza base onto a non-stick baking tray and set aside while you make the topping. This will give the base a chance to rise.

TIP
IF YOU HAVE DOUGH LEFT OVER, RATHER THAN THROWING IT AWAY, PUT THE DOUGH BALLS INTO AN AIRTIGHT BAG AND THEN FREEZE THEM. THIS CAN BE VERY HANDY FOR WHEN YOU WANT TO HAVE PIZZA AGAIN.

To make the topping

8 Mix the tomato purée, Italian seasoning, crushed garlic, salt, pepper and a dessertspoon of olive oil together.

9 Spread about a dessertspoon of the tomato topping onto the pizza base and sprinkle with chopped mozzarella cheese.

10 Now make the face. Use some olives for eyes, red and green peppers for the nose, mouth and eyebrows. You don't have to follow this exact design, create your own using whatever topping you like.

11 Get a grown-up to preheat the oven to a hot temperature, 220°C/425°F/gas mark 7. Get the grown-up to place your pizza in the oven for about 10 minutes.

12 These are best eaten hot so make sure an adult helps you put the pizza on a plate. Be careful that it's not too hot when you take your first bite.

Pizza Belissima!!!!!

Bravo Sombrero

You will need

For the salsa
2 vine ripe tomatoes
   (these give a more
   succulent flavour
   than ordinary tomatoes)
1 small red onion
1 cup chopped coriander
juice of ½ lime
salt & pepper
1 packet of flour tortillas
   (8 in a packet)
8 slices of cheese

To garnish
½ cup crème fraîche
½ cup natural yoghurt
½ cup fresh coriander

Tools

2 mixing bowls
chopping board
juicer
plate
baking tray
table knife
dessertspoon

1 Carefully chop up the tomatoes with a table knife on a clean chopping board. Put the chopped tomatoes into a mixing bowl.

2 Chop a red onion into small pieces, again using your table knife. Red onion tends to be a little sweeter and gives the salsa a delicious flavour. Always wash your hands after chopping an onion and don't put your fingers near your mouth or eyes because the juice from the onion can sting. Add the onion to the tomatoes.

3 Wash and chop the coriander and add to the mixing bowl.

4 Using a juicer, squeeze half a lime. Don't throw away the other half as you can use that for decoration. Add the juice to the bowl and now a little salt and pepper. Mix it well and leave it sit aside for about an hour. Salsa is better the longer it sits because all the flavours have time to combine together.

5 Lay out the flour tortilla on a plate. Spoon a dessertspoon of salsa onto the edge of the tortilla, then lay a slice of cheese on top and roll up the tortilla. Repeat this for all of the tortillas and then place them on a baking tray.

6 Get a grown-up to preheat the oven to a moderate temperature, 180°C/350°F/gas mark 4. Bake in the oven for about 6 to 8 minutes.

To garnish

7 Mix the crème fraîche, yoghurt and coriander together. Spoon some over the tortilla for a fantastic Bravo Sombrero.

Jurassic Breads

You will need

1 package dried
  yeast
1 dessertspoon sugar
pinch of salt
1 cup with ½ warm water
  and ½ milk
2 dessertspoons sunflower
  oil
3 to 4 cups strong white
  flour
raisins
1 egg

Tools

large mixing bowl
small mixing bowl
baking tray
cup
wooden spoon
dessertspoon
pastry brush

1 Stir the yeast, sugar, salt and the cup of milk and water in a mixing bowl. Make sure the water is lukewarm as this will help the yeast to rise.

2 Add the oil and mix well with the wooden spoon. Do not add the oil before this stage because if you do the yeast will stick together and not rise.

3 Add 2 cups of strong white flour. At this stage you might find it a little difficult to mix, so instead of using a wooden spoon start mixing with your hands. Keep adding a little flour, depending on how sticky the mixture is.

4 Knead the bread in the bowl using your knuckles, this means push and stretch it to make sure the ingredients are well mixed in. Once you have formed a dough ball, remove it from the bowl and continue to knead on a flat work surface using some flour to stop it from sticking. Push and fold for about 5 minutes until it is soft and elastic and has a silky texture.

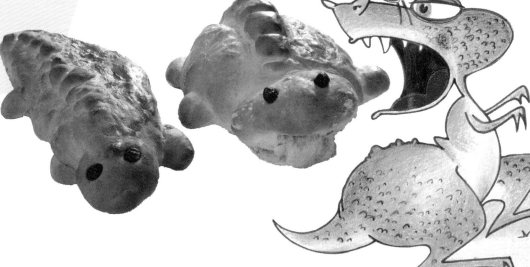

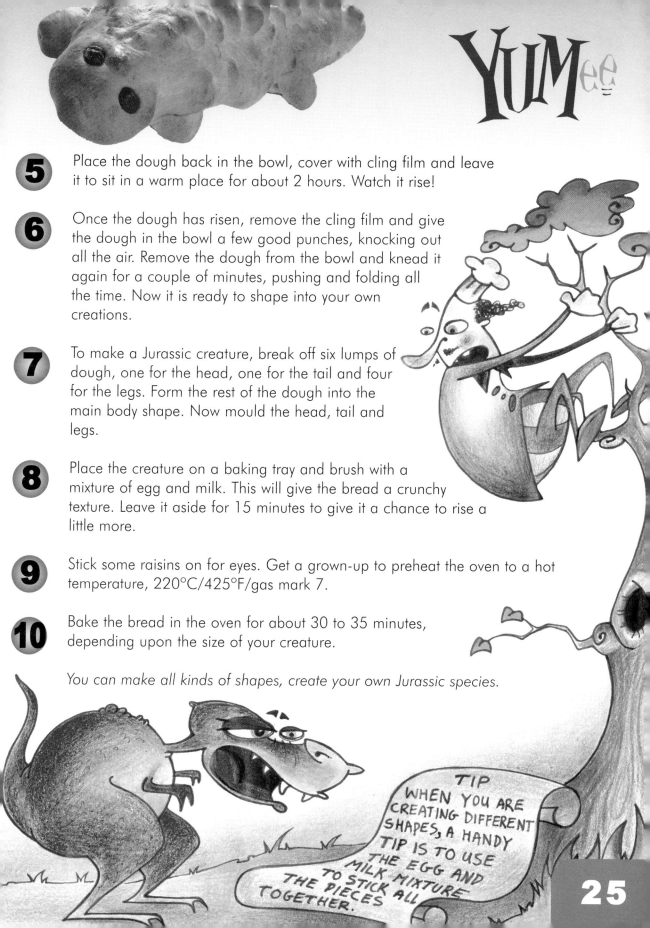

YUMee

5 Place the dough back in the bowl, cover with cling film and leave it to sit in a warm place for about 2 hours. Watch it rise!

6 Once the dough has risen, remove the cling film and give the dough in the bowl a few good punches, knocking out all the air. Remove the dough from the bowl and knead it again for a couple of minutes, pushing and folding all the time. Now it is ready to shape into your own creations.

7 To make a Jurassic creature, break off six lumps of dough, one for the head, one for the tail and four for the legs. Form the rest of the dough into the main body shape. Now mould the head, tail and legs.

8 Place the creature on a baking tray and brush with a mixture of egg and milk. This will give the bread a crunchy texture. Leave it aside for 15 minutes to give it a chance to rise a little more.

9 Stick some raisins on for eyes. Get a grown-up to preheat the oven to a hot temperature, 220°C/425°F/gas mark 7.

10 Bake the bread in the oven for about 30 to 35 minutes, depending upon the size of your creature.

You can make all kinds of shapes, create your own Jurassic species.

TIP
WHEN YOU ARE CREATING DIFFERENT SHAPES, A HANDY TIP IS TO USE THE EGG AND MILK MIXTURE TO STICK ALL THE PIECES TOGETHER.

Jolly Juices

You will need

apple juice
cranberry juice
orange juice

To decorate
kiwi
orange segments
white sugar
juice of ½ lemon

Tools

ice cube trays
tray or lid of a container
zip lock bag or plastic bag
tea towel
rolling pin
drinking glass
2 saucers
dessertspoon
table knife
cocktail sticks

1 To make the frozen juice cubes, place ice trays onto a larger tray and pour in different types of juice. Using a larger tray will help you to contain any spills. Use as many juices as you like. Put the ice trays into the freezer and leave for at least 4 hours.

2 To empty out the ice cubes, run a little cold water over the ice tray just to loosen the cubes and then empty them into a tray or the lid of a container. This stops the ice cubes from going all over the place.

3 Next get a zip lock bag or, if you don't have one, just use a plastic bag. Put the ice cubes into the bag and close tightly. Don't mix up the different cubes, keep them separate.

4 Place a tea towel on a work top. Put the plastic bag in the middle of the towel and place another tea towel on top. Now for the fun part. Take a rolling pin and give the bag a few good wallops to smash the ice cubes.

5 Get a nice drinking glass and dip the rim of the glass into a saucer with lemon juice and then into a saucer of sugar, frosting the top of the glass.

6 Using a dessertspoon, put some of each of the different flavours into the glass, building up a rainbow of frozen juices.

To decorate

7 Wash and slice a kiwi and an orange and place them on the rim of your glass. Get yourself a nice big straw and sluuuurrp away!

TIP
INSTEAD OF USING AN ICE TRAY, USE ICE CUBE PLASTIC BAGS. POUR THE JUICE INTO THE BAG THROUGH A FUNNEL. TIE A KNOT IN THE TOP AS INSTRUCTED ON BOX AND PLACE IN FREEZER.

Pirate Potatoes

You will need

1 large potato
1 dessertspoon
  cream cheese
2 dessertspoons
  chopped cheese
  (use your favourite)
½ teaspoon mustard
salt
pepper
tin baked beans

To decorate
red pepper
sliced cheese
cocktail stick

Tools

baking tray
fork
table knife
tablespoon
cocktail sticks
plate

1 Wash and dry a large potato and place it on a baking tray. Get a firm grip on the potato and carefully pierce the skin several times with a fork, this stops the skin from cracking as it cooks.

2 Get a grown-up to put the potato into a moderate oven, 180°C/350°F/gas mark 4, for an hour and a half.

3 Let the potato cool down for a while and then cut it in half lengthways using a table knife. It is very important that you let the potato cool as it can be very hot. Cut a little off the under side of the potato because this will help it stand on the plate.

4 Use a tablespoon to scoop out the centre of the potato into a mixing bowl.

YUMee

5 Add the cream cheese, chopped cheese, mustard, salt and pepper to the potato and mix well with a fork.

6 Spoon the mixture back into the potato skin and really stuff it in using the back of the dessertspoon to give yourself a good foundation to build your boat.

7 Place the potato back onto the baking tray.

8 Get a grown-up to help you with the oven and bake the stuffed potato at a moderate temperature, 180°C/350°F/gas mark 4, for about 15 minutes.

To build the mast

9 Use a table knife to cut the stalk off the red pepper, scoop out the seeds and throw them away and then cut the pepper into triangles.

10 To make a mast and sail, stick a large cocktail stick up the centre of a red pepper triangle. You could also use a cheese triangle.

11 Place the mast in the centre of the potato.

12 Get a grown-up to help you heat a plate of beans. Place the pirate ship on top of the bean sea.

The best thing about these is that you get two pirate boats out of one potato, so they are great to make with friends or for parties.

TIP
WHEN SCOOPING OUT THE POTATO MAKE SURE TO LEAVE A LITTLE OF THE POTATO AROUND THE INSIDE CLOSE TO THE SKIN. THIS KEEPS THE SKIN OF THE POTATO STRONG AND WILL STOP IT FROM SPLITTING. YOU DON'T WANT YOUR BOAT TO SINK IN THE BEAN SEA.

Silly Spaghetti

Buon gusto!

You will need

500g vine ripe
  tomatoes
1 teacup fresh
  basil
1 teacup fresh parsley
2 dessertspoons olive oil
2 dessertspoons pine nuts
a clove of garlic
salt and pepper

Tools

chopping board
table knife
garlic crusher
large mixing
  bowl
fork
dish that can go in the
  microwave
dinner plate

1 Chop the tomatoes into small chunks on a chopping board with a table knife. Put them into a large mixing bowl.

2 Peel and crush the garlic using a garlic crusher, if you need help ask a grown-up. Do not put your fingers anywhere near your eyes or mouth after handling the garlic as it can sting. Make sure to wash your hands. Add the garlic to the tomatoes.

3 Chop the parsley and basil on a chopping board with your table knife and add them to the tomatoes.

4 Add the olive oil, salt and pepper and pine nuts. Make sure to ask an adult if you can eat nuts because some people can be allergic to them. If you don't have pine nuts you can use any soft nut like walnuts or the monkey nuts you get around Halloween.

5 Use a fork to give the tomatoes and all the other ingredients a good mix, mashing them up with the fork.

TIP IF YOU HAVE ANY OF THE MIXTURE LEFT OVER, DON'T THROW IT OUT. STORE IT IN A JAR OR CONTAINER. A GLASS JAR IS BETTER FOR KEEPING THE LOVELY FLAVOURS AND FRESHNESS OF THE SAUCE. IT SHOULD LAST IN THE FRIDGE FOR 3 DAYS.

YuMee

6 Get a grown-up to help you heat some pasta. If you are heating up leftover pasta in the microwave, sprinkle with a little water first so it does not dry out and heat at a moderate temperature for about 1 minute.

7 Be very careful at this stage because the pasta can be a little hot. Spoon the pasta onto a plate and put about 2 dessertspoons of sauce on top. You can put as much or as little as you like.

8 To finish the dish, garnish (decorate) it with some fresh basil or parsley by placing a little sprig on top of the sauce.

Bellissimo!!!!!!
If you like cheese you can sprinkle some chopped cheese on top.
The sauce is great on toast and even better if you use it as a dip
for crackers or crisps.

SpoolyOOly

You will need

6 oranges
1 lemon
1 tin of raspberries
1 litre white lemonade
1 litre sparkling water

To decorate
orange slices
fun party straws

Tools

large punch bowl or
    mixing bowl
chopping board
juice squeezer
table knife
party cups
ladle or teacup

A delicious fruity, fizzy drink, great for parties.

1 Get a grown-up to open the tin of raspberries. Put the raspberries into the punch bowl and mash them with a fork.

2 Squeeze 5 oranges and a lemon using a hand squeezer. This may take a little muscle. Put all the juice into the punch bowl.

3 Cut the last orange into slices using a table knife. Put these slices into the punch bowl.

4 Add 1 litre of white lemonade and 1 litre of sparkling water to the fruit.

5 Using a ladle or teacup, scoop out the punch into large glasses or party cups.

To decorate

6 Put an orange slice on the rim of the glass and drink through a fun party straw.

TIP
INSTEAD OF SQUEEZING THE ORANGES, YOU COULD USE A CARTON OF PURE ORANGE JUICE.

Raspberry Bread

You will need

8 slices of white
    bread
500ml milk
250ml cream
3 eggs
150g sugar
1 teaspoon vanilla essence
½ teaspoon cinnamon
250g fresh raspberries
    (washed)

Tools

chopping board
table knife
2 large mixing bowls
wooden spoon
whisk
baking dish
sieve

1 On a chopping board, remove the crusts from the bread with a table knife and cut each slice into four pieces.

2 Put the bread into a large mixing bowl, pour in the milk and stir with a wooden spoon. Leave the bread aside to soak for about an hour.

3 Whisk the eggs in another large mixing bowl and gradually add the sugar. Stir in the cream, vanilla essence and cinnamon.

Pudding

4. Mix the egg mixture and bread together with a wooden spoon.

5. Now add the washed raspberries and mix it all together.

6. Grease a baking dish with a little butter and carefully pour in the bread mixture.

7. Get a grown-up to preheat the oven to a moderate temperature, 180°C/350°F/gas mark 4.

8. Bake the pudding in the oven for about 45 minutes.

To decorate

9. Sieve some icing sugar on top of the pudding. This pudding can be eaten warm or cold and is very nice with cream.

TIP
INSTEAD OF MAKING A LARGE PUDDING, IF YOU HAVE LITTLE OVENPROOF DISHES (RAMEKINS), YOU CAN MAKE INDIVIDUAL PUDDINGS. THEY ONLY TAKE ABOUT 25 MINUTES TO BAKE, BUT DON'T FORGET TO GET AN ADULT TO HELP WITH THE OVEN.

Tralee Toasties

You will need

150g tomato purée
  (from a tube)
1 dessertspoon
  olive oil
1 garlic clove, crushed
½ teaspoon Italian seasoning
4 slices of bread
salt and pepper
4–6 slices cheese

For the vegetable kebab

red and green pepper
some mushrooms

Tools

mixing bowl
dessertspoon
pastry brush
non-stick baking tray
table knife
cocktail stick

This is a great idea for a snack or lunch, simple and yummy. You will need the help of a grown-up when using the oven.

1 Mix the tomato purée, Italian seasoning (oregano and basil), crushed garlic, salt and pepper and a dessertspoon of olive oil in a mixing bowl. This is your secret sauce.

2 To make two sandwiches use four slices of bread. Using a pastry brush, brush olive oil on both sides of two slices of bread, these are the top slices. Brush olive oil on only one side of the other slices and place these oil side down onto a non-stick baking tray. Spread one dessertspoon of the secret sauce onto these slices.

3 Now add the cheese, 2 slices for each sandwich.

4 Put the other slice of bread on top to make the sandwich.

36

5 Wash and chop red and green pepper into chunks with your table knife. Wash and remove the stem from the mushroom. Carefully skewer each one with a cocktail stick, you may need a grown-up to help you.

6 Place each kebab on the baking tray with the sandwiches. Brush each kebab with olive oil and season with salt and pepper.

7 Get a grown-up to help you at this stage. The sandwiches need to go into a hot oven, 220°C/425°F/gas mark 7, for about 8 minutes. This allows enough time for the cheese to melt and the bread to toast.

8 These are best eaten hot so make sure a grown-up helps you put the sandwiches onto a chopping board to cut them into smaller, finger-size sandwiches. Be very careful as the cheese can be very hot.

You can also add other fillings like ham, salami or even use different types of cheese.

TIP
IF YOU DON'T HAVE A PASTRY BRUSH YOU CAN RUB THE OLIVE OIL ON THE BREAD BY USING A DESSERTSPOON. ALL YOU DO IS SPOON A LITTLE AT A TIME AND SPREAD IT AROUND.

Roly Poly

You will need

For the pastry
180g plain white flour
120g butter
1 teaspoon sugar
a large pinch of salt
ice cold water

For the filling
4 jumbo sausages
3 green onions
a small apple
some chopped parsley
salt and pepper

Tools

2 large mixing bowls
table knife
teaspoon
rolling pin
non-stick baking tray
chopping board
tablespoon
small mixing bowl
pastry brush
fork
weighing scales

To make the pastry

1 Put the flour, sugar and a pinch of salt into a large mixing bowl. Using a table knife chop the butter into small chunks and then add them to the bowl. Use your fingers to work the butter into the flour until it turns into crumbs.

2 Spoon a few teaspoons of cold water into the crumbed flour and butter and mix until it turns into dough. If you find it too sticky just add a little flour. A secret to good pastry is that the less you have to handle it the better it turns out.

3 Flour a large clean work surface area and, using a floured rolling pin, roll out the dough to about the thickness of a wooden spoon. Add some more flour if it becomes too sticky. Place the pastry onto a non-stick baking tray and set aside until the filling is ready.

For the filling

Always clean your hands before and after you handle raw sausage meat.

4 Using your table knife, slice through the skin of the sausages, this works best if the sausages are cold from the fridge. Squeeze the sausage meat into a large bowl and throw away the skins.

5 On a clean chopping board chop the green onion using a table knife. Add this to the sausage meat.

6 Get a grown-up to help you at this stage. Peel and chop a small apple and chop the parsley with your table knife. Add these to the sausage meat along with some salt and pepper.

7 Mix well using a tablespoon.

To combine

8 Beat an egg and a little milk in a small mixing bowl. Brush this mixture onto the edges of the pastry with a brush. This will help the pastry stick together so the filling doesn't fall out.

9 Spoon the sausage mixture onto one half of the rolled out pastry and then fold over. Cut away any excess pastry and mash the edges together with a fork. Score the pastry with a table knife (this means cut little lines in the top of the pastry). This allows the air to escape and prevents the pastry from exploding! Now brush the top with some egg and milk mixture, this will make it brown and crispy.

10 Get a grown-up to place the Roly Poly into a moderate oven, 180°C/350°F/ gas mark 4, for about 35 minutes until the sausage meat is cooked through.

11 When it comes out of the oven, leave it to cool before you cut it into little slices.

Serve with some salad or spaghetti hoops.

39

Fruity Fools

You will need

1 cup cream
250g frozen
   raspberries
2 tablespoons sugar

To decorate

1 kiwi fruit
orange segments

Tools

2 large mixing bowls
whisk
chopping board
sieve
dessertspoon
wooden spoon
serving dish or dessert
   bowl

1 Whisk the cream in a large mixing bowl until it is stiff and forms peaks.

2 Separate the fruit from the juice using a sieve.

3 Add the sugar and the raspberries in the sieve to the cream and mix together using a wooden spoon. Instead of stirring the mixture, fold it in by scooping around the edges of the bowl. This helps to keep the mixture creamy. Add a little of the raspberry juice from the other bowl but not too much, you want it to be thick and creamy rather than runny.

4 Use a dessertspoon to spoon some of the mixture into a dessert bowl. You should get about four normal portions with this amount of mixture.

TIP
FOR EXTRA SPECIAL
FRUITY FOOL,
CRUMBLE SOME
BISCUITS OR
CHOCOLATE
MALTED BALLS
ON TOP. IT
TASTES GREAT
WITH CRUNCHY
BITS.

To decorate

5 Decorate using some orange segments and slices of kiwi fruit to make your Fruity Fools even more colourful.

Hazelnut Sweets

You will need

400g ground
   hazelnuts
200g caster sugar
2 eggs

To decorate

25g dark chocolate
whole hazelnuts

Tools

large mixing bowl
whisk
tablespoon
2 teaspoons
baking tray
baking paper
bowl that can go in the
   microwave
sweet papers
weighing scales

Hazelnut Sweets are not only good for parties, but they also make a great present. All you need to make a nice gift is an old sweet box or even a nice little bag.

1 Whisk 2 eggs in a large mixing bowl.

2 Add the sugar and hazelnuts to the eggs and mix with a tablespoon until the mixture becomes gooey.

3 Line a baking tray with baking paper.

4 Use two teaspoons to scoop out the mixture onto the tray, one to scoop and the other to slide the mixture off the spoon. You should get about 20 little sweets from your mixture.

5 Get an adult to help you with the oven. The sweets need to go into a hot oven, 200°C/400°F/gas mark 6, for about 15 minutes.

6 When they come out of the oven leave them aside to cool.

To decorate

7 Get an adult to help you melt the chocolate in the microwave.

8 Dip the top of each sweet in the chocolate. Be careful as the chocolate can be very hot. Place a whole nut on top and leave until the chocolate hardens. When they are ready, wrap the sweets in sweet papers.

Rhubarb Clafouti

You will need

250g rhubarb
  (about 2 medium
  stalks)
2 eggs
175ml cream
100ml natural yoghurt
2 dessertspoons golden
  syrup

Tools

small baking dish
chopping board
table knife
large mixing bowl
whisk
dessertspoon
weighing scales

Cibo bello del Gran Paradiso!

1 Rinse the rhubarb and use a table knife to cut off the tops of the stalks. Cut the rhubarb into small chunks on a chopping board.

2 Put the rhubarb into a small baking dish.

3 In a large mixing bowl whisk the eggs, yoghurt, cream and golden syrup. It should reach a sort of custard stage.

4 Pour the mixture over the fruit. Jiggle the dish a little to make sure the mixture goes into all corners of the dish.

5 Get a grown-up to help you with the oven and bake the clafouti in a moderate oven, 180°C/350°F/gas mark 4, for about 30 minutes. Let your adult helper take the dish out of the oven and leave it aside to cool for a while.

6 Spoon the Rhubarb Clafouti into smaller dishes to serve.

Instead of rhubarb you could try raspberries or blueberries.

Sanger Rolls

You will need

4 slices of bread
1 hard boiled egg,
    peeled
1 teaspoon
    mayonnaise/salad cream
pinch of salt/pepper
½ teaspoon curry powder
chopped parsley
1 chopped red pepper
1 packet of cheese and
    onion crisps

Tools

mixing bowl
table knife
chopping board
fork
rolling pin
dessertspoon

1. Place the peeled, hard boiled egg into a mixing bowl and cut into little bits using a table knife. This will make it easier to mash.

2. Add salt, pepper, curry powder and mayonnaise.

3. Carefully chop the parsley using a table knife and chopping board and add this to the egg.

4. Mix it all together using a fork.

5. Remove the crusts from the bread using a table knife. Roll the bread flat with a rolling pin. Don't throw the bread crusts away, you can put them in a plastic bag and feed them to the ducks.

TIP. HERE'S A GREAT TIP TO MAKE THEM LOOK MORE IMPRESSIVE. GET AN EGG BOX SMALL ENOUGH TO FIT INTO YOUR LUNCH BOX. PAINT IT WITH YOUR FAVOURITE COLOUR. USE SOME PAPER CASES AND PLACE THE LITTLE ROLLS INTO THE EGG BOX. THIS WAY YOU CAN SEPARATE SWEET FROM SAVOURY.

6. Spread a dessertspoon of the egg mixture onto the bread and add some red pepper and crushed crisps.

7. Roll the bread up into a little Swiss roll. You should get about four rolls from this amount of egg mixture.

8. Cut the roll into three finger-size rolls and place them in your lunch box.

You can use other types of filling, try ham and cheese, smoked salmon and cream cheese or everyone's favourite, peanut butter and jam.

YUMee Cake

Tá fáinne an lae níos fearr le císte agus té.

You will need

125g butter
½ cup sunflower oil
100g unsweetened chocolate
1 cup water

350g flour
300g sugar
1 teaspoon baking powder
1 teaspoon cinnamon
3 eggs

Tools

mixing bowl that can go in
  the microwave
weighing scales
sieve
wooden spoon
10-inch cake tin
baking paper

1 Get an adult to help you melt the chocolate and butter in the microwave. Be careful when you are melting butter in the microwave as it can burn very easily. So make sure you use a low setting on the microwave. Get the grown-up to give it a stir.

2 Add the oil and water to the melted chocolate and butter.

3 Beat the eggs with the melted chocolate, one at a time ('beat' means to stir something very, very quickly).

4 Measure the flour on a weighing scales.

5 Sieve the flour, baking powder and cinnamon into the chocolate mixture. Mix well using a wooden spoon.

6 Get a 10-inch cake tin and line the bottom and sides with baking paper.

7 Pour the cake mixture into the tin.

8 Get a grown-up to help you to bake the cake in a moderate oven, 180°C/350°F/ gas mark 4, for about 30-35 minutes. After it has cooked, leave it to cool for about 30 minutes. This really helps it set.

To decorate

9 Cut out the YUMee stencil from the back of this book and stick a little sticky tape on the front as this will help you lift it from the cake. Place the stencil on the cake leaving the sticky tape facing up. Using a sieve, sprinkle some icing sugar over the top. Remove the stencil and you are left with a YUMee cake.

TIP
YOU DON'T JUST HAVE TO USE A YUMee STENCIL, YOU CAN CUT OUT ANY SHAPE YOU LIKE. OLD GREETING CARDS ARE GOOD FOR STENCILS - CHRISTMAS, VALENTINE OR BIRTHDAY CARDS ARE GREAT FOR PICTURES.

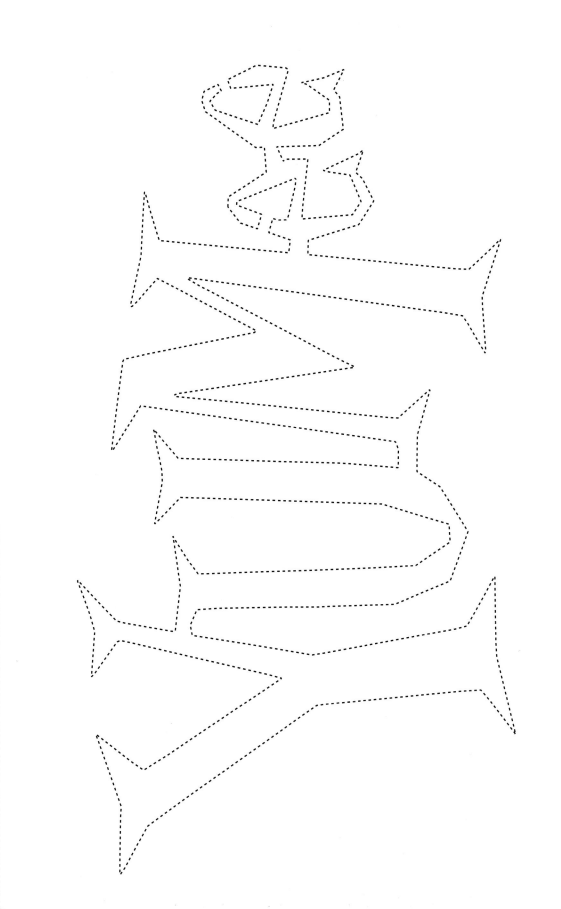